The Hundred-Year Barn

The Hundred-Year Barn

words by PATRICIA MacLACHLAN

illustrations by KENARD PAK

KATHERINE TEGEN BOOKS
An Imprint of HarperCollins Publishers

The hundred-year barn was built one summer in our meadow
with a small stream running through.

It was built by townspeople:
fathers and daughters,
mothers and sons,
grandmothers and grandfathers,
and friends.

I was only five years old, and I held my mother's hand and watched.

"See, Jack? The horses are working hard," said my mother.

I watched the horses pull wagons of brush away.

The builders cleared the land to lay a foundation of gray stone.

Day after day our friends built wooden frames, leaving spaces
for windows that my father would admire when the light fell across
his butterscotch floors.

They raised the frames—side after side, up and up—and climbed tall ladders to bolt them tightly to the chestnut beams.

The sun rose hot.

The cows, horses, and sheep ate grass under the shade trees and watched, too.

Sometimes we played by the meadow stream, jumping over it, laughing. One day my friend Martha fell in, which made us laugh more. It wasn't deep, so we all got in the stream and sat down with her.

My father lost his wedding ring, a plain gold band.
Everyone looked for it.
I was the smallest and I found it in the grass. I put it in my
pocket, but it fell through a hole.

They searched for days.

It was never found.

"We're still married," my mother said to my father.

My father smiled.

"Now I'm married to the barn, too," he said.

When I walked out into the meadow with my older cousin Emma, she pointed to the meadow's edge. A red fox sat there, half hidden by tall grasses.

Swallows flew down and then up again, ice-blue wings flashing in sunlight.

"The swallows wait to nest in the barn," said Emma.

The barn boards were nailed. The roof shingles were nailed. The sound of hammering echoed in the valley like the beat of music.

And after many days, when the building was done, Emma climbed a ladder and placed a pine bough at the peak.

Everyone cheered.

They ate food at long tables set with vases of wildflowers.

Salads and breads and cakes.

They drank cider made from my father's apples.

After lunch I fell asleep under the table.

A photographer took a picture of all those who helped build the barn.

My father raised a glass and thanked his friends for a summer's work.

"The barn will be called the hundred-year barn," my father said.

"May it last a hundred years or longer! And more than a hundred of you helped build it. Cheers to you all!"

Later, my father would nail the photograph up on a barn wall.

He wrote under the picture:

The Hundred-Year Barn Builders
August 1919

It took a long time to finish the inside of the barn.

There was a loft for hay and bins for grain.

They built stalls for the horses and a space for the hay cutter and baler.

There was a pen for the cows and one for the sheep so in winter they would be warm.

On the very last day of summer the barn was painted red.

Seasons went by.

The cows were milked.

I was old enough to help with the milking, morning and evening.

The horses pulled the plow and the cutter and the baler.
Sometimes I rode on the cutter with my father.

When the horses' work was done, they ran in the meadow
and drank from the stream and rolled in the grass.

Barn lambs were born. And calves with snow-white faces.
They followed me in the field and ran when I ran.

Once, a lamb named Baby pushed me over and licked my face
with his little tongue.

The swallows swept in and out and in again, building
their nests on barn ledges. Just like Emma had told me
when I was little.

When the cousins came to visit, we slept in the barn in our
sleeping bags, reading by lantern light and laughing in the dark.
"You tell scary stories, Jack," said one cousin.

When it began to rain, a possum with a baby on her back
sat in the doorway and waited for the rainstorm to end.
We watched her until we fell asleep.

The barn cat, Tillie, slept with us.

Tillie sometimes caught mice, but when the mice played dead she got bored. What fun was a dead mouse? She didn't care. She was well fed.

She watched us make hay paths and houses in the barn.

More years passed.
I grew older and went away to school and came
back home to help run the farm.

There were weddings in the barn.

My cousin Emma was married in a bright yellow
dress with flowers in her hair.

I married Martha, who had fallen into the stream
years before.

There were birthdays.
And Fourths of July.
Babies were born.
New children played in the barn, making hay houses.
Sometimes they slept in sleeping bags, reading by lantern
light and whispering in the dark.

The mice and barn rats watched them, and when the children slept, the mice crept up to eat crumbs of cookies and cake.

Above them a barn owl, high in the rafters, watched the children sleep and the scurrying of mice.

More time passed.

Tillie's kittens and grand kittens played in the hay and slept in the sun. Chickens strutted in and out of the barn like colorful queens, pecking at grain.

Joe, our hound dog, watched them.

Some nights Joe howled at the moon—a soulful sound.
And the barn owl and her owlets looked down from high rafters.

In winter winds sometimes roof shingles flew away. Sometimes tree branches hit the windows and broke the glass.

But the sheep and cows and horses were warm in winter, out of the snow and the wind and the cold.

Then, when spring came, we would replace the shingles and the window glass.

And when it was warm and the barn looked worn,
we painted it red again.
    It was as beautiful as the day it was built.

"My father called you the hundred-year barn," I said one evening. "Because you will stand for a hundred years or more."

It was a moonlit night and I picked up the broom to sweep the floor. Joe walked in with me, sniffing at something lying on the barn floor.

"What is that, Joe?" I asked.

I looked down and picked up a nest made of sweet
grass and the fur of animals.

It had fallen from the rafters. And the moonlight shone
on something small in the nest.

Something round.

Something gold.

Something I had lost many years ago.

My father's wedding ring.

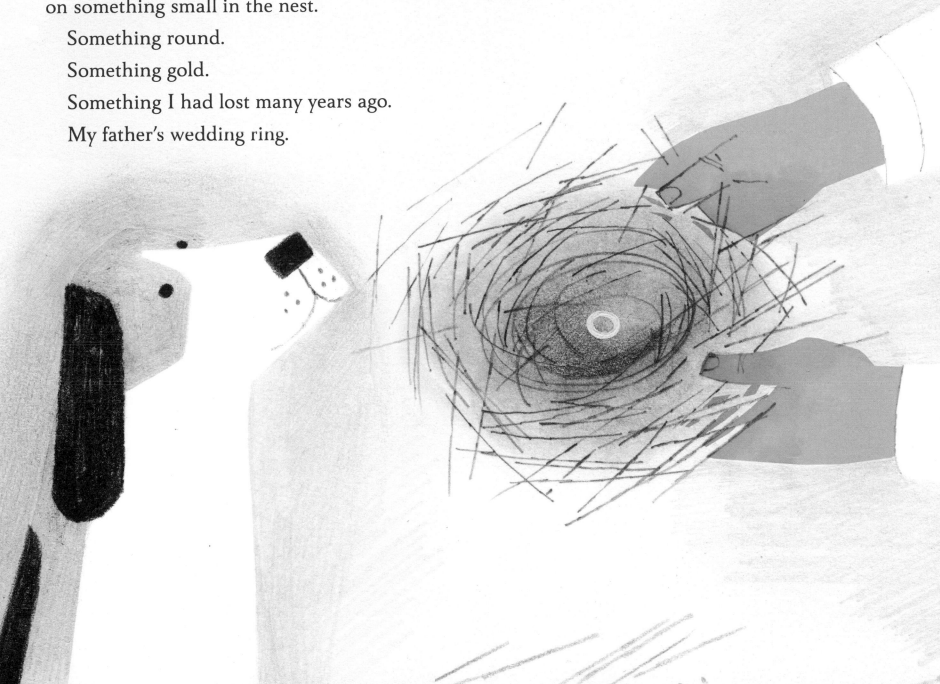

I looked up at where the barn owl had perched.
All these years she had looked down on everything:
the animals,
the children,
in the quiet,

in the sun,
in the dark.
Maybe she saw something from long ago.
Safe for all these years in the barn.

I put the ring on my finger and swept the floor, smiling.

And before I left the barn to sleep, I hung
the wedding ring on a hook beneath my father's
photograph of—

the Hundred-Year Barn.

For my grandparents Eleanora and Johann, Germans out of Russia, who
came to Ellis Island and to the North Dakota prairie —P.M.

For my father, who worked hard these many years —K.P.

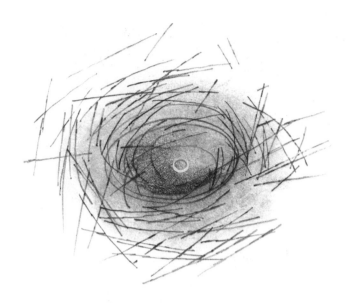

Katherine Tegen Books is an imprint of HarperCollins Publishers.

The Hundred-Year Barn
Text copyright © 2019 by Patricia MacLachlan
Illustrations copyright © 2019 by Kenard Pak

Library of Congress Control Number: 2018952185
ISBN 978-0-06-268773-9

The artist used watercolor, gouache, pencil, ink, and digital media to create the illustrations for this book.
Typography by Aurora Parlagreco and Cara Llewellyn
19 20 21 22 23 SCP 10 9 8 7 6 5 4 3 2 1

First Edition